Catherine and
the Lion

by Clare Jarrett

Carolrhoda Books, Inc./Minneapolis

Published by arrangement with HarperCollins Publishers. The
author/illustrator asserts the moral right to be identified as the
author/illustrator of the work.

This edition first published in 1997 by Carolrhoda Books, Inc.

First published in England in 1996 by HarperCollins Publishers Ltd.,
London.

Carolrhoda Books, Inc., c/o The Lerner Group
241 First Avenue North, Minneapolis, MN 55401

LIBRARY OF CONGRESS CATALOGING-IN-PUBLICATION DATA

Jarrett, Clare
   Catherine and the Lion / by Clare Jarrett.
      p. cm.
   Summary: Catherine is comforted by the company of her imaginary lion
friend, who goes to school with her and accompanies her in all her at-
home activities.
   ISBN 1-57505-035-8
   [1. Imaginary playmates—Fiction. 2. Lions—Fiction. 3. Schools—
Fiction.] I. Title.
PZ7.J2953Cat   1997
[E]—dc20   95-53745

Printed in Hong Kong
Bound in the United States of America
1 2 3 4 5 6 – JR – 02 01 00 99 98 97

Catherine woke up and saw the lion.
He was smiling.

"Hello, Lion," she said.

Lion walked over
and sat next to her.

Catherine told him
about her jungle
gym and her new
sister.

"Let's have breakfast," said Catherine.
They went downstairs. Catherine found
an extra large bowl for Lion.

After breakfast she went to get dressed. She decided to wear her pink dress with yellow buttons.

She put it on as quickly as she could. Then she put on her coat.
"Will you come to school with me?" Catherine asked.

"Yes," said Lion.

She remembered to take
her library book.

At school, she took off her coat and hung it on her peg.

"This way," she whispered and went into the classroom.

"Hello, Catherine," said Mrs. Tickle. The children were pleased to see Lion. Catherine sat between Jason and Lauren, and Lion sat behind her.

"Good morning, everyone," said Mrs. Tickle.

"Good morning, Mrs. Tickle," said the children.

In the morning Catherine did
cutting and pasting, then painting.
She made a picture of Lion.

At recess they skipped and played,
running round and round on the grass.

Lion gave rides.

"I'm thirsty," said Lion.

Catherine found a bowl and
filled it with water for him.

After lunch everybody took a nap. They all lay on mats while Mrs. Tickle read to them. The afternoon was spent making things.

Catherine made a golden crown
and gave it to Lion.

"Thank you, Catherine," said Lion.

When it was time to go home,
Catherine gave Lion a big hug.

"I like school," she said.
"So do I," said Lion.

On the way home they did some shopping. Catherine chose jewels, two silver bracelets and a diamond ring.

Catherine felt tired. Lion gave her a ride some of the way.

They played in the yard. Lion rocked Catherine in the hammock and began to teach her how to roar.

Soon supper was ready.
It was fish sticks.

"My lion is under the
table," said Catherine.

After supper they watched ZAPCAT.
Then it was bath time.

Lion sat next to the bath
and sniffed the steam.

Catherine wrote LION
on the window.

He watched Catherine
put on her pajamas and
brush her teeth.

"Lions don't have to brush
their teeth," he said.
"Of course they do," said
Catherine. "Everybody does."

"Say good night to little sister,"
said Catherine.

Mom read Catherine a story, tucked her in, and gave her a big hug and kiss.

"Night, night, darling," she said. "Sleep tight." Catherine snuggled down.

"Good night, Lion. Will
you always be here?"

"Yes, I will," said Lion.